THE RECKONING

STEPHANIE SCISSOM

Available from Black Hare Press

Edited by D. Kershaw
Formatting by Ben Thomas
Cover design by Dawn Burdett

Twitter: @BlackHarePress
Facebook: BlackHarePress
Website: www.BlackHarePress.com

For Selena and Chase.

I love you always.

Stephanie Scissom, February 2021

TABLE OF CONTENTS

CHAPTER 1

Josephine looked up at the sound of crunching gravel as Grant's truck carefully rumbled up the driveway. He wasn't about to cross her mother again. She couldn't even hear the radio this time.

Lyndsey leaned out the passenger window and yelled, "Hi, Mrs Meeks!"

Josephine's mother sighed, then yelled, "Hi, kids!" To Josephine, she said, "Be home by 11, okay?"

"Yes, Ma'am!"

She kissed her mother's cheek and ran to the truck. Lyndsey jumped out to open the third door and Josephine piled in next to Devin. His grin gave her butterflies. Her summer had certainly got more exciting since Lyndsey had introduced them at the swimming hole a few weeks ago.

"Any word on your ATV?" Grant asked.

Josephine frowned. "Nope. Not a thing. I can't believe someone stole it the very first week we got it."

Devin shook his head. "Lots of pillheads around here now. They steal what isn't locked down."

Lyndsey fiddled with her phone. "Okay, are y'all ready to play? We all have to think of an intent—"

"Wait, what was this called?" Josephine asked.

12

"Explain it to me again."

"It's called Randonautica. The app asks you to think of an intent, then it gives you random local coordinates. You're supposed to go and explore, see if you can find what your intent was. These kids in Seattle were playing it and they found a body stuffed in a suitcase."

"I think there were multiple bodies and suitcases," Grant said. "It operates on chaos theory, that these random points cause a ripple in the matrix and cause unusual things to happen."

Devin snorted and muttered, "The Matrix," under his breath. To Josephine, he said, "Basically, it's like a Ouija board game. You ask scary stuff and psych yourself out."

Lyndsey twisted to glare at him. "It doesn't have to be scary. We could say, 'I want to find something purple' or 'I want to see a puppy'."

"Ah, no." Devin winked at Josephine. "If we

do this, I want to do 'ghost'."

Lyndsey grinned. "Me, too. Okay..." She tapped on her phone and looked at Grant. "So, I pick anomaly?"

"Yeah, or void, either one."

"Anomaly, then ANU... Now, everyone concentrate and think 'ghost'. 1...2...3..."

Josephine was still thinking about her ATV and the look on her mother's face when she discovered it stolen.

It's worth a shot, she thought, then focused on 'something that was taken from me'.

"Here we go!" Lyndsey handed Grant her phone.

"3.2 miles to a ghost. Who knew?" He turned up the radio. Soon, they were all shouting the chorus of "Copperhead Road" along with Steve Earle.

Grant turned down the radio at the end of a long, gravel drive. "Hey, I think I've been here before. There's this really cool swing."

"Dude, this is private property," Devin said. "We better turn around."

"No one lives here," Grant replied. "And they don't have signs posted. If I remember, they have a couple of picnic tables beside the swing. I don't think they'll care as long as we don't hurt anything or leave any trash."

"I don't know." Josephine could just imagine her mother's reaction if they went to jail.

"C'mon," Grant said. "We can say we were lost, turning around."

The whole time, he'd been driving slowly, watching the point on the map.

"It's beautiful here," Lyndsey said, as a small brown house with a rusted tin roof came into view. Like Grant stated, there were two picnic tables and a long rope swing beside the bluff. At the highest arc, it would probably feel like you were swinging into eternity.

"The yard's mowed," Devin said, as Grant rolled to a stop and Lyndsey bailed out. She opened the third door and tugged Josephine out, pulling her toward the stop.

"Hold up!" Grant yelled. "Dev, come here."

Together they climbed on the swing and tested the ropes, jumping up and down.

"That would be a hell of a crash if the rope broke," Grant mused. "I think it's good, but don't go crazy."

Devin was still looking around. The yard *was* freshly mowed, but the place looked deserted. Devin took the phone from Grant's hand and looked at the house.

"Well, the ghost is in there. And if it doesn't come out and offer us tea, we won't meet, because deserted or not, I'm not breaking in there."

"Agreed," Josephine said.

He handed her Lyndsey's phone and pulled out his own to snap pictures.

"My sister thinks she's a ghost hunter," he explained to Josephine, as Grant pushed Lyndsey on the swing. "She says always take lots of pictures, even if you don't see anything, and look at them later to see if anything turns up."

Josephine looked around but didn't feel uneasy. The home was modest and in need of repair, but it was a lovely area. Lush green grass, tree-lined drive, and of course, the spectacular bluff view that was growing increasingly more impressive as the sun began to set.

Grant was on the swing now, whooping as he soared high into the orange and pink skyline. "This is amazing!" he cried.

In a few minutes, he slowed and used his feet to scoot to a stop. "You're up, girl," he said.

Hesitantly, Josephine climbed on the swing. It

felt sturdy enough, and she would have to swing pretty high to be in danger, she thought, but it still felt disorienting to be this close to the bluff. Devin gave her a push.

"Not too high," she pleaded, and he complied.

The sunset grew bolder, painting the sky with violent shades of orange, red, and pink. She turned her head to tell Devin to take a picture of it when her gaze caught something on the back porch of the house.

A man—watching them. She could see straight through him.

Josephine screamed and nearly fell backwards out of the swing. She felt Devin's hands grabbing at her, trying to slow her down as he yelled and asked her what was wrong.

She glanced away for just a second as he finally wrestled the swing to a stop, and when she looked back, the figure was gone.

"Let's go, let's go!" she cried and wouldn't tell them anything until they were in the truck and heading down the driveway.

"I saw something. A ghost. On the back porch."

Grant slammed on the brakes. "For real? Let's go back."

"No! Take me home."

When he hesitated, Devin said, "Dude, she's scared. Let's go."

Lyndsey twisted in the seat to look at her, eyes huge. "Well, what did he look like? Was he in old clothes, like a civil war uniform or something?"

"No…he was wearing a blue flannel shirt and jeans. He looked like he was older than us, early twenties. Dark hair, light eyes."

"Did he have any wounds you could see? What was his expression?" Grant asked.

"No, and he was just staring. He didn't look

mad or scary."

"Then why were you screaming?" Grant said.

"Because I could see right through him."

They went to the local hamburger place instead of going home and discussed it in hushed tones in the back booth. Grant might have persuaded her to go back, but the sun was down now, and there was no way Josephine intended to be there after dark.

Later that night, Josephine lay in her bed, trying to sleep. Considering that someone had just recently broken into the garage near her bedroom to steal the ATV, and thoughts of the apparition she'd seen that afternoon, she was still awake and checking her social media at 3:00 a.m. when Devin messaged her.

Hey, I saw you were online. Are you okay?

Yes, she replied. *Why are you up?*

I was looking over the pics I took today

and...nvm I'll tell you tomorrow. You've had enough excitement.

That got Josephine's attention. *You can't leave me hanging. Tell me.*

It took a little more wheedling, but finally, he sent her a picture. It was a shot of the house. Immediately, she looked at the back porch but saw nothing out of the ordinary.

She typed *?*

Zoom on the right window. Top part, second pane.

She did and nearly dropped her phone. It looked like the side of a face staring out at them, partially obscured, with a glowing eye.

Josephine turned on her bedside lamp, but it did nothing to help the queasy feeling in the pit of her stomach.

Holy crap! She typed.

Ikr? I nearly pissed myself when I saw that.

You see what I see?

A face...

LOL I sent it to Grant and Lyndsey earlier. Lyndsey said she made her little sister get in bed with her. The pic's pretty cool, huh? And creepy, for our first randonaut. I'm going to post it on Facebook.

Don't tag me. My mom would die if she thought we were playing around with stuff like that.

Josephine didn't sleep at all until the sun came up.

CHAPTER 2

Charlie's phone buzzed as he walked in his front door after work. It was a text from his cousin, Jennifer.

Looks like Travis' old house is famous. The kid who posted it didn't name a location, but I thought I'd give you a heads-up in case people start poking around and some damn idiot falls off the bluff there. I can send Ralph over to post some No Trespassing signs if you want.

She sent him a screenshot of the post, which was made at 3:46 a.m. and had over 500 likes and 200 comments. Charlie looked at the picture first and saw nothing. He cursed when he zoomed and saw the face, then he read the caption.

So you think some crackhead is living in that old place? He texted.

Naw, Jen replied. *I think it's a trick of the light. Doesn't look like much of anything to me.*

It did to Charlie though, and the thought of someone going through Travis' things incensed him, even though he knew his brother was never coming back for them.

Do you want us to post it for you?

No, he replied. *I'll head up. I need to check on Ma'am anyway.*

Although he'd originally planned to work that day, Charlie found himself so aggravated that he made a few phone calls, threw some clothes in a bag, and headed out that afternoon.

The drive from Huntsville, Alabama, to Beersheba Springs, Tennessee, took less than two hours, but the trip felt endless. Charlie decided to go to Travis' old place first, before he went to his grandmother's. He parked his truck at his grandpa's old barn, grabbed his shotgun from the seat, and headed across the hollow to Travis' house. He didn't want to alert anyone who might be squatting there.

It took him awhile to find the spare key, but he finally dug it out of the corner of the overgrown flower bed. A glance inside made him feel a little more at ease. Though he paid Jen's kids to mow in the summers and knew she occasionally did some light housework while they were working, it was apparent no one had been in here for a while. The only footsteps marring the dust on the worn, wooden floor were his own. He walked over to the window where he thought he'd seen the face in the window. The dust was undisturbed there. He couldn't figure out what would have looked like a face in the window, unless, as Jen had suggested, it was some trick of the light.

It hurt to be back in here. He hadn't been inside here in nearly seventeen years now, since Travis had first gone missing and he'd let the sheriff in to poke around. But they had both known, even then, that Travis hadn't been the one who had anything to hide. All those sins had fallen on Charlie.

All this stuff should've been packed up years ago, but Ma'am had insisted on keeping it waiting for him. Truthfully, it had given Charlie some comfort to pretend he might come back as well, even though Charlie himself had left and rarely been back since.

He touched a picture of the two of them that

hung on the wall. Smiling, bare-chested, scrawny little shits, but they'd thought they were big deals then. Raised by grandparents after their parents had abandoned them for their oxycodone habits, they at least had each other.

Charlie heard a radio, and the sound of a vehicle approaching. He tightened his grip on the shotgun and peeked out the window at the red pickup pulling up.

CHAPTER 3

Josephine gazed at the house with a trepidation that didn't ease, even when Devin took her hand. She wished she hadn't let Grant talk her into coming back, but he'd promised to get them out before dark. He'd felt it might be important to come back around the same time of day, but the setting sun made her anxious.

This time, when they got out of the truck, no

one headed for the swing. They all stared at the house. Devin took a few pictures, then he ventured closer.

"No!" Josephine said and grabbed his arm.

He gave her a reassuring smile and shook her hand loose. "I'm not going in. I just want a look at the porch."

She hung back with Lyndsey while Grant went to peer in the window and Devin walked around to the back porch. Devin started up the steps, then froze, lifting his hands in the air. She heard the unmistakable sound of a shotgun racking.

"Please, Mister," he said. "Don't shoot."

"Back off the porch, slowly," a male voice said. "Tell your friend to get his ass around here where I can see him."

Devin tried to yell Grant's name, but his voice cracked. Josephine was fumbling for her phone to call 9-1-1 when the man came into view. Stunned, she dropped her phone and almost reached for it, but Lyndsey nudged her sharply and they both lifted their hands in the air.

The man held the shotgun at his side, not pointing it at Devin, but not looking like he'd hesitate to use it, either. He looked exactly like the apparition she'd seen yesterday, except his hair was blond, and he was definitely not transparent.

Grant came around the side of the building, his hands also in the air.

"Someone want to tell me what the hell you're doing on private property?" the man asked, as Devin moved to stand in front of her.

"Spread out," he said. "I want to see your hands at all times."

"We're sorry, sir," Devin babbled. "We don't mean any harm and weren't going to bother anything."

"Then why were you on this porch?" The

man's eyes swung to Josephine, and he looked startled. "What's your name?" he said. "Who's your kin?"

"She's not from here, sir," Devin said. "She moved here at the start of summer."

"It's this app," Grant blurted. "You know, like on a phone."

The man sighed. "I know what an app is."

He was older than Josephine first thought. Maybe close to forty. His face still held tension, but he seemed more annoyed than angry.

"It's like, a scavenger hunting app," Devin said.

"And what could you possibly scavenge here?" he asked.

"Uh, this sounds dumb, but I swear it's the truth. We were goofing off, looking for ghosts. Josephine thought she saw one on the porch yesterday, so we were just investigating. Taking a few pictures. If you let us leave, I swear we will never come back."

"You got that right." He scowled. "I should call the cops."

"Please don't, sir," Devin begged. "Our parents will kill us."

The man looked from Josephine to Lyndsey. "I saw the picture on Facebook. That's your ghost?"

"No, sir," Josephine choked out, her throat dry. "I saw something on the back porch, when I was on the swing."

"A ghost," he all but snorted. "Did it look all…" He fluttered his free hand by his ear and made a face.

"No," she said. "It looked like you, except his hair was dark and I could see through him."

The transformation of the man's face was truly terrifying. Shock to pure, unadulterated rage. He snatched a phone from his back pocket, punched in three numbers, then growled, "I need an officer at 533, Utah Road. I've got trespassers."

Josephine was almost relieved he was calling the police on them. He looked so angry for a moment that she was sure he was going to murder them.

No one said a word until the police arrived. The female officer who walked up first greeted the blond man, "Well, hell, Charlie Johnston. I haven't seen you in years!"

"Kris," he said, his face relaxing. He made no move to stop her as she took the shotgun by the butt and carried it over to prop it against the house. Then she hugged him.

"Looking good! Still in the army?"

"Out for a year now."

She glanced at them. "So, you have some trespassers? Out here on the swing."

"I don't give a shit about the swing. I've never

tried to stop anyone from coming here to that. But these kids were on the front and back porches and I don't know what they were figuring on doing, but this is what pissed me off."

He motioned her closer to the house, out of their earshot. Josephine looked at Devin, who gave her an "I don't know" shrug.

The cop's eyes narrowed, and she looked at them as mean as the Charlie guy had.

"Alright," she said and motioned to the officer in the second car that had rolled up behind her. "You take the boys, and the ladies can ride with me. Let's go down to the station and sort this out." Looking at Charlie, she asked, "You need a ride?"

He shook his head. "I left my truck down by the barn. I'll meet you there in a minute."

Lyndsey looked pale and her hand was icy as she reached to squeeze Josephine's hand in the back of the squad car. "My mom is going to kill me," she said softly, but somehow the officer heard her.

"You should've thought about that before you go poking around a man's house and then try to prank him. I don't blame him for being mad. That's an awful thing to joke about."

Josephine and Lyndsey looked at each other, confused.

"Prank?" Lyndsey said. "I don't know what you—"

"Save it for your mama," she said. "Travis was an old friend of mine, and I don't appreciate your joke any more than Charlie did."

At the station, the officers sat them down and made them call their parents. That was probably the hardest call Josephine had ever had to make. Her mother said surprisingly little, however, other than a terse "I'm on my way."

Charlie Johnston arrived as she hung up the phone, and he glared at her again. He looked at her like he wanted to say something, but then he turned his head and asked the female officer about her family and how they'd been.

Josephine's mom arrived first. Charlie gave her a startled look and said, "Rosalee?"

Josephine's mom actually paled and touched the wall, as if to steady herself. "Charlie?"

He stood and crossed the room to embrace her. Awkwardly, her mom hugged him back. Josephine wasn't used to seeing her so rattled. She almost looked…scared.

"That one." He pointed at Josephine. "That one's yours."

Her mother nodded. "That is Josephine. What—what's going on?"

"Let's wait on the other parents," the officer said.

When they arrived, Officer Kris ushered them into a conference room and pointed at Lyndsey.

"You. You like to talk. Tell us what you were doing on Mr Johnston's property."

Haltingly, Lyndsey told them about the app and showed it to them on her phone. She told them everything, up until the point they first met Charlie Johnston.

Charlie leaned back in his chair and looked at Josephine. "Who told you about Travis? None of you are old enough to know about him. Who told you to say that to me? Be honest and we can all walk out of here right now."

Josephine looked at her mother. "Mama, I don't—"

"Look at Mr Johnston," her mother said. "He's the one who addressed you. And tell him the truth."

Tears burned her eyes. "Please, Mr Johnston, I don't know what you're talking about. I don't know what I saw, but it scared me. I saw a man, about your height, a little slimmer, who looked a lot like you.

He was just standing there looking at us, but I—I could see through him."

Charlie muttered something under his breath, but she continued, "He was wearing a blue and black flannel shirt, jeans. Some kind of black work boots, with silver tape across the toes."

Charlie and Officer Kris exchanged a sharp look.

"I was scared and trying to stop the swing. When I looked away and looked back, he was gone," she said, unable to stop the tears rolling down her face. "I know it sounds crazy, or like I'm lying, but that's what I saw."

"Did any of the rest of you see this 'ghost'?" the officer asked, and they all shook their heads.

She looked at Charlie and lifted her eyebrows. Then she said, "Adults, please step into the hall with me. Kids, stay put."

CHAPTER 4

Kris looked at Charlie and said, "Do you want to press charges?"

He looked at Rosalee and sighed. "No, of course not. Just tell them to stay off the property."

"Oh, you can be sure of it," one of the boys' fathers said and shook his hand. "Thank you, Mr Johnston. I'm terribly sorry. I promise you, it won't happen again."

The other parents murmured similar assurances and went to collect their kids. Kris caught Rosalee's arm. "Hold up," she said. "We want to talk to you about something."

After the others left, Kris said, "The thing that was most concerning to Mr Johnston was Josephine's description of the 'ghost'. The outfit she described him in, down to the tape he wore on his boots, was what he was wearing the night he disappeared, back in 2002."

Rosalee gaped at her, then at Charlie. For a long moment, she said nothing, then she stammered, "Josephine wasn't even alive then. How…what…" She gasped, "Surely you don't think I had anything to do with Travis' disappearance, or Josephine's father, God rest his soul. He's been dead for nearly eight years now. There's no way—"

"No," Charlie said immediately. "Of course there's not. I just don't know how she'd know that.

It unnerved me."

Someone called for Officer Kris, and she said, "Be right back," and walked down the hall, leaving Charlie and Rosalee alone.

Rosalee said, "I have no explanation to give you, but I promise I will talk to her about it."

"I don't believe in ghosts," he said.

"Oh, neither do I," she said quickly. "You know such things were never taught at our house."

He pictured the stern Reverend Turner. "No, I know they weren't. I heard he passed a few years back. He never liked me much, but I wouldn't have liked some punk dating my daughter either." He cleared his throat. "How *is* Emma? Does she still live around here?"

Rosalee nodded. "Yes. She lives in Warren County, works as a nurse at the hospital down there. She straightened up, went to college, made a nice life for herself."

"Good," he said, and meant it. Emma had been his first love, but they'd both been wild as hell and no good for each other at all. Still, he'd felt guilty for how he'd ended things with her, but his grief over Travis had nearly destroyed him. Travis had been in Charlie's truck that night. Charlie would go to his grave wondering if whoever had taken his brother that night had done so, thinking it was him. He had had many enemies back then, owed many debts. Travis had not.

"How are your grandparents?" Rosalee asked.

"Papa died three years ago. Ma'am is in the nursing home. She doesn't know us much anymore." He gave Rosalee a pained smile. "That's why I don't come back here often. Other than Jen and her family, I'm pretty much alone now."

She squeezed his hand, her eyes shining. "I'm so sorry. I want you to know, I'm proud of you. I used to be so scared you'd never make it out of your teens, but apparently, you've built a good life for yourself as well. Travis would be proud, too."

Charlie couldn't speak over the lump in his throat, but that was okay, because Kris was back.

"Let her go?" she asked Charlie, and he nodded.

"When I saw you walk in, I knew which was yours. She looks just like your mom and Emma."

The door opened, and the girl came out first. Unlike the other kids who'd hurried past him, murmuring the apologies their parents demanded, she looked him dead in the eye and said, "I really am sorry, Mr Johnston. I have no explanation for what I saw, but I won't trespass again."

Charlie watched them leave, his thoughts troubled. He did not believe in ghosts, but he also did not believe this girl was lying to him.

CHAPTER 5

"Mama, say something," Josephine pleaded. "I'm sorry. And I really did see what I said I saw."

"I want you to delete that app. I can't believe you went looking for ghosts. Your grandfather would've been horrified."

"I didn't use 'ghost' as my intention," Josephine said. "I was thinking of something else."

"What were you thinking of?"

47

"The ATV. I asked for 'things that were taken from me'."

Her mother looked rattled again, taking her eyes from the road to look at her, then jerking the car back when she hit the rumble strip. She remained silent for the rest of the ride.

Figuring she'd give things time to cool off, Josephine kissed her mother's cheek and went upstairs to her room. As she reached the top of the stairs, she heard her mom on the phone. Probably telling Aunt Emma what she'd done.

Josephine had a dozen missed texts from Lyndsey and Devin.

Devin: *Hey, I found some info on your ghost*

He sent her a link to a newspaper article. The first thing she saw was the Missing photo. It *was* him.

Josephine: 😶

Devin: *Look at the description of what he was*

wearing. It's just like you said.

The article asked the public for any information on the whereabouts of Travis Johnston, 22, last seen at a residence on Briar Ridge Road, where he picked up his brother from a party. After taking his brother home to his parents' residence on Utah Road, he announced he was returning to his own home, also on Utah Road. A relative found a red pickup registered to Mr Johnston's father in the driveway the next morning, still running with the driver's side door open.

Josephine: *Devin, what have we gotten into?*

CHAPTER 6

Back at Travis' house, Charlie couldn't stop thinking about the kids' story. He typed "randonautica" in a search engine and read some articles. From what he gathered, it was something of a Magic 8 Ball cloaked in confusing garble about quantum random number coordinates and "breaking the matrix." The user thought or spoke of an intent, such as love, or cat, or ghost, and then set out to explore with coordinates given. He watched a video of some kids in Seattle who had supposedly found a body in a suitcase while playing with the app.

Charlie didn't believe in that sort of thing, not one bit. If Travis were actually here, why would he appear to a bunch of kids he didn't know instead of his own brother?

Maybe because they asked. Maybe it has something to do with the app.

Feeling like a complete and utter dumbass, he downloaded the app. It took him a few minutes to figure out the differences between anomaly, attractors, and voids, then he had to look up ANU and temporal. When it asked him for his intent, he muttered, "Where's my brother?"

Maybe the coordinates *were* randomly generated, because it didn't give him Travis' house, or anywhere close to it. Still feeling dumb, but equally restless, he hit start on the directions and jumped in his truck.

He found himself across town, on Briar Ridge Road, which dead-ended at a pool hall just past the Richardson place. Jason and Austin had been his best friends back in the day. It was their house that Travis had dragged him from that night. Charlie had been high, but he still remembered some of the awful things he'd said, ending with "Fuck you," when Travis had unceremoniously dumped him in their grandparents' yard and told him to sleep it off. It killed him to know those were the last words he'd ever say to Travis. He'd thought Travis was trying to control him back then, but now realised that his older brother had only been trying to look out for him, to keep him from turning out like their parents had. Charlie hadn't seen their mom since he was five, and he supposed his dad was back in jail, since he hadn't tried to hunt Charlie down asking for money recently. They had lived with their grandparents, but Travis had taken care of him up until the day he'd gone missing.

Charlie slowed as the GPS told him he was approaching his point. It stopped him a quarter of a mile from the Richardson place, and there was nothing but woods on either side. Still, he decided to play it out, so he parked on the side of the road, climbed out, and walked.

The sun was setting, and the forest grew darker, blocking out the brilliant orange sky. Four hundred yards into the pine thicket, his phone announced he'd reached his destination. Charlie looked around. Even though he'd found exactly what he'd expected to—nothing—he still felt bitter disappointment. No ghost in worn-out steel toes, nothing that looked suspicious at all.

As he returned to his truck, he saw an old beat-up Honda slowing to check him out. It stopped in the middle of the road as Charlie approached.

A gaunt-faced man stuck his head out the window and said, "You lost, Buddy? This is a dead-end—Charlie, is that you?"

The man gaped at him, and it finally dawned on Charlie who he was. Jason Richardson, looking a good twenty years older than Charlie knew him to be. The facial tattoos didn't help matters.

Charlie's shock probably showed on his face, because Jason frowned. Charlie forced a smile. "Jason! I'll be damned. How've you been?"

"Man, I ain't seen you in, what, 15 or 16 years? What are you doing back in town, and way out here?"

"Closer to 17. I came to visit Ma'am and Jen and was just riding around. Had to stop to piss."

Jason gave him a long look, and Charlie could bet he probably had some pot planted nearby, if not a lab. But then Jason gave him an awkward, close-lipped smile.

"I gotta get going now," he said. "Take care."

He pulled out and Charlie did a U-turn in the road and followed him out. Seeing Jason made him think of Travis again, and the life his brother had ultimately saved him from. He just wished Travis could see that he had amounted to something.

Charlie pulled into the old Amoco station at the end of Briar Ridge Road and went in to get something to drink. The woman behind the counter glanced up, then did a double take.

"Oh, my God. Charlie Johnston, is that you?"

He squinted at her, then smiled. "Caitlin?"

She gave him a big grin. "Let me look at you! My goodness, it's been awhile."

Caitlin's father owned this station. She had been a friend—maybe more—to Travis back in the day. Though she smiled, he saw the sadness in her eyes when she looked at him.

They chatted for a while, asking about each

other's families, then she said, "Travis offered to come back and sit with me until my shift ended." She laughed. "His exact words were 'Let's ride around and run my gas out of Charlie's piece of junk truck.' I told him no, to get home because he had to work the next day. I wish I'd said yes."

Charlie looked at her, confused. "We didn't stop here that night."

"I meant when he came back."

"What are you talking about?"

It was Caitlin's turn to look confused. "You mean the sheriff never told you? I called him the next morning when your truck was found in Travis' driveway. Travis came walking in here around 11:30, carrying a gas can, cussing your old truck. He said the gauge was stuck on full or something and he ran out of gas about a half a mile that way," she said, pointing to Myers Town Road.

The gauge on his old truck *had* done that.

Charlie's heart thumped in his ears. It had been so long since he'd had any new information.

"He said he'd left his wallet and toolbox in the back of his truck and he had to have it for work. He asked if he could charge his gas and run the money back by. Of course, I said yes. He pumped eight even and promised he'd be back, but I never saw him again. He probably just forgot, but I worried about him that night. That wasn't like Travis."

Charlie stood frozen, trying to process it. Travis' toolbox had still been in the truck he'd left parked at the pool hall, Charlie was sure of it. His wallet had never been found.

He fished his own wallet out of his back pocket, and Caitlin tried to wave him off. "Oh, no, I don't care about the money. I was just wondering if something had happened when he went back to get his truck."

Charlie peeled off a five and three ones and put

them on the counter. "Take it. Travis would've wanted his debt paid. And I don't know about the other, but I'm going to find out."

Travis' old truck, like his house, had been carefully preserved since his disappearance. It now resided in a barn beside his grandparents' house. Charlie let Jen know he was there, then went to check it out.

He found the dented red toolbox that Travis had carried to work daily in the front passenger floorboard. Then he fished beneath the foam in a hole in Travis' seat until his fingertips grazed something hard. Travis liked to stick his wallet there during the workday, because he moved so much climbing off and on the logging equipment, he feared losing it.

Charlie gazed at it, then flipped it open. Travis' face, so much like his own, gazed at him from his driver's licence. An insurance card that expired in January 2003, a couple of ticket stubs, and a debit card were squeezed beneath his licence, and the inside pocket, a neatly folded picture of him and Caitlin on his tailgate and one hundred and twelve dollars.

So Travis had never made it back—or had decided not to—return to his truck. It didn't make sense. He would need both the toolbox and wallet for work the next day. Yet, Charlie's truck had been found in Travis' driveway.

Maybe he had forgotten the keys, Charlie thought, but then remembered to check the frame rail. Travis kept a spare key in a combo lockbox there. It was also still intact.

Charlie raised up and nearly collided with a shadowy figure coming round the side of the truck. It was all he could do not to scream like a little girl.

"Boo!" she said, then covered her mouth. "Oh God, no. I didn't mean…"

"Emma?" he said. "Is that you?"

Before she could answer, he seized her in a bear hug. She laughed and squeezed him back just as hard.

"What are you doing here?" he asked.

Her smiling face made him feel happier than anything had in a long, long while. Even in the dim light of the barn, she was lovely. He'd thought he was too old for sparks, but Emma stirred up the same feelings for him that she had at seventeen.

"Rosalee told me you were in town, and I just had to come see you."

"I'm so glad you did," he said and hugged her again.

She made no move to pull back, wrapping her arms around his waist and resting her head on his shoulder. He lost himself in the perfumed smell of her hair.

"I heard what happened at Travis' today," she

said. "I'm so sorry. Josephine is a good kid—"

"It's okay," he said, pulling back to look at her. "Just rattled me. And I still can't explain it. She was describing Travis. Down to those old raggedy-ass boots he wouldn't replace because they were so comfortable."

"I never told her anything about him. None of us did—"

"No, I felt like she was being sincere. But I don't believe in ghosts, Em, and I don't understand what's going on."

He leaned against Travis' truck and told her everything that had happened since he'd arrived in town.

"Wow," she said. "So, do you think he argued with someone at the pool hall, and they followed him back home?"

Charlie shook his head. "I don't know. No matter what happened, I don't know why he wouldn't have got his wallet and toolbox. You know how he was."

He glanced at the motorcycle in the corner. Ralph maintained all the vehicles here, the motorcycle being no exception. Looking at Emma, he said, "Feel like taking a ride?"

Soon, they were roaring down Myers Town Road for his second time that day. Riding that bike, with that girl on its back, holding on tight, Charlie almost felt like he'd slipped through a hole in time, when his only worry was getting Emma back home before her daddy came looking for them.

He stopped at the Amoco and fuelled up, then gave Caitlin the photograph. She cried when she looked at it and thanked him.

Back on the road, he slowed to show Emma where the app had pointed him, but it was so dark by now that they didn't get off to explore. The next stop was the pool hall at the end of the road.

It was a little more than a shack, a ramshackle building with three pool tables that hadn't been exactly level even in their prime, but he and Emma had spent a lot of time here, and at the small white house just before it, where Jason and Austin had grown up. Charlie was somewhat surprised it was still open, but it was lit up with colourful Christmas lights across the porch, even in mid-June. Marshall Tucker blared from the jukebox as they removed their helmets and climbed from the bike. Charlie took her hand without even thinking much about it, and they walked inside. The seven occupants inside all stopped to stare—the four young people blankly, the two older ones like they'd seen a ghost.

The couples turned back to their games, while the other two continued to stare. The younger of the pair stood and took a faltering step.

"Charlie? Emma?" he gasped, then barrelled towards them, seizing them both in a hug.

"Austin!" Charlie said. "Long time, no see."

"No shit!" Austin said happily. "You guys look great! What are you doing here?"

As with Jason, the years of drugs and alcohol hadn't been kind to Austin, but he had retained his same friendly personality, it seemed. He called over his shoulder to the old man by the beer cooler. "Uncle Moss, look who it is!"

The proprietor's face creased into a toothless grin. "Well, I'll be!"

The old man had sold them beer and weed, sometimes a little more in their youth. He climbed off his stool to come shake Charlie's hand. "Well, ain't you a sight for sore eyes."

They made small talk for a few minutes, talking about the military and their lives. Austin pulled out his wallet to show them a picture of a little blonde-haired girl who he said was his daughter, Gemma.

Then Charlie looked at Austin. "The night that Travis went missing, after he dragged me out of your house and took me home, did he come back here?"

Austin gave him a surprised look. "No, not that I know of. Did you see him, Moss?"

The old man shook his head. "The sheriff asked me that, back when it happened, but I never saw him if he did. I'm sorry, boy. I hated that for y'all."

"Yeah." Austin looked at his shoes. "Me, too. You were a good friend, Charlie. I've missed you."

He looked almost like he was going to cry, and Charlie surprised himself by giving him another hug. He and Emma declined their offer of a beer and said they had to get going.

Austin followed them to the door, his face sad. Charlie felt sorry for him, knowing his world had never been bigger than this town.

"That was awkward," Emma said, as Charlie reached for their helmets. "Where are we going now?"

He smiled. "I don't know. But I was hoping now that I'd got the prettiest girl in Grundy County back on my bike again, that she'd let me keep her for a while."

Her phone buzzed, and she checked her messages. "Ooh, looks like Rosalee and Josephine are making s'mores. You want to go get some?"

Charlie hesitated. "I'm not sure they'd want me there. I was pretty grouchy to your niece today."

Emma twisted her phone around for him to read. The message said: *Bring Charlie to the house. We're making hotdogs and s'mores.*

"Sounds like an invite to me," she said with a shrug.

"Well, okay," he said. "I've never been known to turn down a s'more or a chance to hang out with you."

He raised his arms to put her helmet on, but something in her eyes made him hesitate. Charlie set it back down on the seat and kissed her. Her lips were as soft and sweet as they'd been at seventeen, and she kissed him just as fervently as she had back then.

"I'm really glad you're here," she said.

She directed him to Rosalee's house, where they found her sister and Josephine sitting around the firepit in the front yard. The girl looked surprised to see him, and Charlie felt guilty for pulling a shotgun on her and her friends today.

Emma took his hand and tugged him forward.

"Aunt Emma...on a motorcycle?" Josephine said, looking at her mother.

"Am I that old?" Emma laughed. "I've ridden quite a few miles on this one, with this guy. Did your mom tell you Charlie was my old boyfriend?"

Josephine gaped at them, then at Rosalee. "No, somehow she forgot to mention that."

"There are hotdogs in the cooler there, along with water and soft drinks. Everything else is on the table behind you. Help yourselves. Charlie, do you mind grabbing us some sticks? I forgot to buy prongs."

"Prongs," he uttered with mock contempt and winked at Josephine. "Come on, girl. Let's find some sticks."

They walked to the edge of the woods, where Charlie reached to examine thin little tree branches. He finally found four that were to his liking, broke, cleaned, and handed them to her.

"I'm really sorry about today," he said. "Travis is still a sensitive subject."

"Oh, I totally get it," she said. "And I hope you don't think I'm playing some mean joke. I really saw what I said I did."

Charlie looked at her for a long moment, then sighed. "I believe you, but I've never believed in ghosts. I was all over that place today. Why couldn't I see him?"

"Maybe because you don't believe you can? I don't know."

He looked up to where Rosalee and Emma were talking and watching them from the patio. "I'm trying," he said. "I even tried your app when I got back."

Josephine gave him a sharp look. "Ooh, where did it take you? Did you find anything?"

"It took me to the middle of nowhere," he said, then he realised that it really *had* given him something. If he hadn't have made that trip, he never would've stopped by that station, and he never would've learned what he had tonight, even if it still didn't make sense. He felt like there was something there, some vital clue he was missing.

"I'm sorry," she said, as they started walking back. "I wasn't looking for ghosts either, so I'm not sure why I was the one who saw him."

She told him about her ATV and her intent to find 'something that was taken from me'.

"It's kind of weird though," she said. "There are all kinds of Internet videos about it. People have found some strange stuff."

They stopped talking as they re-joined the women, and Charlie got out his knife to whittle tips on the ends of the sticks. For the first time, he noticed the guitar strapped across the back of Josephine's chair. "You play?" he asked.

She shrugged. "A little."

"I used to play." He handed Emma the sticks, then reached for the guitar. "In fact, I'm willing to bet your Aunt here had something to do with your name. She used to love this song I wrote about a girl named Josephine."

He strummed a few bars and stopped as he tried to remember the lyrics. "Give me a second," he said. "It's been a long time."

When he started singing, Josephine surprised him by joining in. Her voice was sweet, and they harmonised almost effortlessly.

"She used to sing that to me, too," Josephine said. "One question: why are Josephines and Carolines always sweet in songs?"

"You're not sweet?" Charlie asked.

He smiled at Emma, but she didn't smile back. She was looking at Rosalee.

"We could write a song about a mean Josephine, I suppose. 'Josephine, Josephine. She was the meanest girl I've ever seen. Broke my heart, stole my dreams. That mean old Josephine.'"

Josephine laughed. "I gotta say, lyrically, it doesn't hold up to the original."

He gave her a mock scowl. "Well, duh. I wrote

that about my kindergarten girlfriend, and it took me ten whole years to write. Stop pressuring me!"

Charlie expected Emma to laugh, or to at least refute his joke, but when he looked up at her, she was crying. He glanced at Josephine, who looked as surprised as he was, then at Rosalee. She was crying, too.

"I want to say, first of all, that we're sorry," Rosalee said. "Charlie, when I saw you today, and you said what you did, about being all alone, it broke my heart." She looked at Josephine. "And then you said what you said, about your intention for that game. I called Emma when I got home and we decided it was time."

"Time for what?" Josephine demanded, her voice rising. She sounded scared, and suddenly, Charlie felt that way, too, though he had no idea what was happening.

"We never meant to hurt either of you," Emma

said, her voice cracking. "But it was all we knew to do at the time." Looking at Charlie, she said, "You know how my father was. He was furious."

"What are you saying?" Charlie asked, his throat dry.

Emma cried harder. "You were gone. You just left. I didn't know what to do. I could have tracked you down to that rehab place, but you know how we were back then. We weren't ready to be parents."

"I couldn't have kids," Rosalee said. "I'd been trying for two years at that point. Father wanted her to give the baby up for adoption, but I begged him, let me keep it. We lived out of state. No one would ever know she wasn't mine."

Stunned, Charlie looked at Josephine. She stared at Rosalee like a deer caught in headlights.

Rosalee reached for Josephine's hand, but the girl snatched it away. "Terry was a good man, and he loved you like his own. We always intended to tell you the truth one day, but as you got older…it was easier just to—"

"Keep lying to me?" Josephine snapped. "How could you do this?" She glared at Emma. "How could either of you?"

Emma was sobbing. It was hard to even understand what she was saying. "Seeing you together. I realise what we've done. Charlie, I'm so sorry. I feel so selfish. At least I got to see her grow up."

"I hate you," Josephine cried. "I hate you both."

She took off running down the driveway. Both Rosalee and Emma shouted her name, but she never slowed.

Emma started after her, but Charlie caught her arm. "I'll get her."

"But—"

Charlie glanced at her, then Rosalee. "You've

done enough. I've got her."

He took off on his motorcycle to catch her. She had her head down, crying, when he pulled up beside her. He held out a helmet.

"I'm not going back there."

"I'm not asking you to."

She looked at him, then took the helmet. Snapping it under her chin, she climbed on behind him. Charlie sped off down the highway.

He had a daughter.

His mind could barely process it. He couldn't really be mad, because for a long time he'd scarcely been able to take care of himself—much less a teenage bride and a baby. He truly believed that if he hadn't left this town, he would be dead by now. So he couldn't judge them for doing what they'd done. It just hurt. The girl holding onto his waist was grown, and he knew little more about her than her name.

He didn't want to take her to his grandparents' house, where Jen and Ralph and a million questions waited, so they went back to Travis' place. They walked out to sit under the streetlight at the picnic tables near the bluff.

Charlie handed her his phone and said, "Text your mom. Let her know you're with me."

"Which one?" she retorted, but took it from him and punched in a quick text.

They sat in silence for a moment, then he said, "I had no idea. At any point, if I had known, I would've been back here. But Emma was right. We were both wild back then. I was nothing but trouble. I left here because my brother was in my truck that night, and I figure he got killed because of something I'd done—someone I owed or someone I crossed. Could've been either. I went to rehab and then straight to the army, because I figured I owed him that much, to become a decent human being. I don't think they intended to hurt either of us. They were doing what they thought was best for you."

"Who were they to decide that, though? As much as Mom—*Rosalee*—preached to me about being honest, she lied to me every day. So did Emma. They didn't check to see if you'd straightened out. They stole from both of us." She scoffed, "'Things that were taken from me.' That's what I asked the app for. No wonder she felt guilty."

They sat in silence for another moment, then Charlie said, "We can't change the past, but do you think...you might want to know me now? I've got to say, I'm pretty excited about this."

Josephine gave a startled laugh. "You are?"

He grinned. "I am. You might have been an accident, but you weren't a mistake. I loved Emma. Never really loved another woman after her. And you seem to be made up of the best parts of both of us. How could I not be excited?"

A pair of headlights appeared at the end of the drive. Josephine jumped to her feet.

"I don't want to talk to them yet. Please. Not until we've had time to talk more. Will you make them go away?"

Charlie thought that was reasonable, and he felt a little irritated they didn't give them more time as well. "Yeah. I will. Go hide around the side of the house."

She disappeared into the shadows, but as the vehicle drew closer, he realised it wasn't Emma and Rosalee. Jason and Austin Richardson parked behind his bike and tumbled out of the battered Honda.

Charlie opened his mouth to tell them it wasn't a good time, when he registered two things: that Austin was crying and that Jason held a gun in his hand. He pointed it at Charlie.

"Man, why did you have to come back here

and start poking around?" Jason demanded. "How did you know?"

Holding up his hands, Charlie started backing away. Away from the house, away from Josephine. Loudly, he said, "I don't know what you're talking about. Just put the gun down and we can talk about it."

Austin began sobbing in earnest. He looked at his brother and said, "Jason, don't do this. This is *Charlie*. He was like our brother. We'll just go to the cops, tell them it was an accident." He looked at Charlie. "It was. We didn't mean to hurt him."

Charlie's breath left him in a rush.

Travis, he realised. *They were talking about Travis.*

"What happened?" Charlie asked Austin. "What did you do?"

It was Jason who spoke. "You have to have guessed some of it already, right? I mean, you walked right out of the woods there. Jesus, I thought I was seeing a ghost for a minute. And then at the pool hall, asking questions."

Charlie said nothing. As he'd hoped, Jason kept talking.

"We went riding around after the party. Man, we were still high. Still drunk. I never even saw him. He had on those dark clothes and was walking on the side of the road, carrying that gas can. He didn't suffer though. He did not suffer. Tell him, Austin. He was dead before we could get out to check on him."

Austin shook his head vigorously in agreement, snot bubbling from his nose.

"I'm sorry for how we had to handle it, but man, you know what would've happened if we'd called the police. We'd still be in jail, and it was just an accident. Could've happened to any of us. Could've happened to you, if he'd not taken you home. We did what we had to do. I didn't want them coming back to the pool hall, asking questions, so I drove your truck back here. I'm sorry, Charlie. And I'm sorry for what I have to do now."

He pulled the hammer back on the gun.

"Stop!" Josephine said. "Put your gun down or I'll put a hole straight through him."

Charlie's heart hammered as Josephine appeared behind Austin, who jerked his hands in the air as she rammed something into his back.

"You ain't got no gun!" Jason said.

"Try me," she said, sounding more mad than scared. "It's his, and I know how to shoot. Drop your weapon."

Had he left the house unlocked? Charlie tried to think of what guns were in there, and if any were even loaded.

She prodded Austin again, hard, and he almost stumbled.

"Jason," he pleaded, but Jason only frowned and centred his aim on Charlie's chest.

Suddenly, the wind picked up. Charlie registered the shocked looks on all three faces before something cold slammed straight through him, nearly knocking him down. Someone screamed. He thought it might have been Jason.

Austin took off running down the driveway, and Charlie shouted at Josephine to get down, just as Jason started firing wildly in his direction. One of the bullets caught him in the shoulder, knocking him backwards. He caught just a glimpse of the ghostly thing rushing at Jason, but it was enough.

Travis.

The last thing he heard was Jason's scream, then Charlie passed out.

CHAPTER 7

"Hey! You alright?"

Travis' voice.

Charlie looked first at the boot that nudged his ribs, then up into his brother's face. Travis smiled down at him, looking real. Looking amused.

"Am I dead?" Charlie asked, and Travis rolled his eyes.

"Not from that shot. You'll be fine. I just

85

wanted to talk to you a minute before the ambulance gets here."

"Josephine!" Charlie gasped and tried to sit up. Travis pushed him back down.

"She's fine. She's already called her mother, and 911." Travis grinned. "She's definitely yours. I haven't seen such a staggering display of Johnston DNA in years. Speaking of which…" He nudged Charlie's rib again. "You've put on a little weight. Starting to look like Doug Lee."

Charlie laughed. "Fuck youuuu!"

Travis laughed, too. "Ain't a chicken wing anymore."

That was what their papa had called him, Charlie the chicken wing. He'd say, "He's all skin and bones, but he's tough, like a chicken wing cooked in the microwave."

"Travis, I'm sorry. You wouldn't have been out there that night, if not for me. I've straightened

86

up. I don't do anything anymore. Don't even drink beer."

"It wasn't your fault. And I know. I've been with you. I was with you in rehab, with you in basic. With you in the barn with my old truck today. I've tried to talk to you, and once I thought you might have actually heard me." He grimaced. "But then you ate at that taco truck, anyway."

Charlie snorted, "Oh God, I wish I had heard that one."

It had been a particularly bad, violent case of food poisoning.

"Ma'am will be with me soon," Travis said. "I'll take care of her, get her where she needs to go. Get everyone together tomorrow, have a big Sunday supper like we used to. She'll like that. And when they find my bones, I want to be cremated and scattered off this bluff here. Tired of being in the ground. Don't give me a funeral and don't be sad.

I'm just fine." He cleared his throat. "I love you, little brother, and I'm proud of you."

"I love you, too."

"Now, rouse on up. You've got other family waiting to talk to you, and you're making them anxious." He winked. "Thank God she looks like her mama."

"Oh, yeah? You want to know who does look like me? You," Charlie retorted.

Travis grinned. "Nah, you look like Doug Lee."

Charlie came to with a gasp, opening his eyes to find Josephine and Emma hovering over him. Josephine held pressure on his wound.

"Oh, thank God!" Emma cried as sirens blared in the distance.

"Jason?" he asked.

"He's dead," Josephine said, giving him a look. "Emma says maybe a heart attack. The other one took off. The police are after him."

"What did you do with the gun? Where did you even get it?"

"Oh," Josephine said, looking embarrassed. She held up her first two fingers and blew on them like she was blowing smoke from a barrel. "Actually, it was a stick, but I dropped it back there."

Charlie didn't know whether to be horrified or impressed. He laughed, remembering Travis' words, and said, "Yep, definitely mine."

The gunshot had been a clean one—in and out, missing bone and anything vital. They wanted to keep him overnight for observation, but Charlie refused both that and the pain medication they offered. They gave him a prescription for antibiotics and told them they'd have to wait until the police talked to them, as was the policy for any gunshot wounds. Josephine asked Emma for a moment alone with him.

As soon as the door shut behind Emma, she said, "Did you see what I saw?"

"You mean the part about Travis' ghost going through me and giving Jason Richardson a heart attack?"

Josephine exhaled. "Yeah, that part. I was afraid you'd say no, that I was crazy."

Charlie winked. "Well, maybe we both are. Genetics, you know. But I'm thinking maybe we shouldn't tell the cops all that, even if Austin does."

She nodded in agreement.

"Travis talked to me. When I was passed out. I mean, it could've been a hallucination, but I don't think I'd call myself Doug Lee even if I was delusional."

"What?" she asked, grinning, and he told her some of what Travis had said.

That night, even though it was late, he talked

to Jen, then called the rest of the family—distant cousins, aunts, uncles. Even if his talk with Travis had been a hallucination, he was going to have that Sunday dinner.

The next day, he and Josephine rode to the nursing home to check Ma'am out for the day. She seemed more cognisant than he'd seen her in years and delighted to meet her new great-granddaughter.

While Ma'am supervised Jen and Emma in the kitchen, Charlie introduced Josephine to the rest of the family. She smiled big when she met the pot-bellied Doug Lee, and Charlie made an "eek" face at her over his shoulder.

It was a good day, filled with family, laughter, and reminiscing. Ma'am looked so happy and seemed like her old self. Charlie was glad he'd listened to Travis, because she passed away that night.

The next day, a hesitant-looking Kris knocked

on his door.

"Charlie, I heard about your grandmother, and I'm so sorry. I'm even sorrier to have to tell you this, but we found what we think are Travis' remains. Austin's kind of a burnout, so it took him a while to find the right spot."

"Where?" Charlie asked, but he already knew.

After she left, Charlie walked across the hollow to Travis' place. He was sitting on the swing when Josephine found him.

"Hey," she said. "You okay?"

He smiled up at her. "Yeah, I think so."

She gave him a push on the swing, and he laughed.

"I've been thinking about what you said, and I'm kinda excited about this, too."

"Oh, yeah?" he said.

"Yeah. And I definitely think you need the song writing help."

"What if it takes me another ten years?" he asked.

Josephine shrugged. "I guess we've got time."

ABOUT THE AUTHOR

STEPHANIE SCISSOM hails a small town in Tennessee, where she developed her love of reading and writing and a particular love of southern ghost stories. A Halloween enthusiast, she enjoys traveling to historical spooky locations and investigating the unknown.

In the past 17 years, Stephanie has been published in multiple genres-- romantic suspense, erotica, horror, paranormal, and comedy.

She is one of the founders of the Writing, Prompts, and Critiques Facebook writing group, created in 2017 to foster a supportive, safe, and fun environment to help other writers reach the goal of publication.

Bibliography

She's traditionally published four novels under the name Michelle Perry, with some shorter pieces listed below.

A CONTRACT OF WORDS, Scout Media, 2018

A FLASH OF WORDS, Scout Media, 2019

A MONSTER TOLD ME BEDTIME STORIES, Soteira Press, 2020

ANGELS, Black Hare Press, 2019

APOCALYPSE, Black Hare Press, 2019

BAD ROMANCE, Black Hare Press, 2019

BANNED, Black Hare Press, 2020

BEYOND, Black Hare Press, 2019

BONES, Black Hare Press 2020

STEPHANIE SCISSOM

CAMPFIRE EDITION, Nocturnal Sirens, 2020

CIRCLE OF MAGIC, WPC PRESS 2020

DAUGHTERS OF DARKNESS, Blair Daniels, 2018

FAMILY EDITION, Nocturnal Sirens, 2020

FOLKLORE, Zuma Press, 2019

FOREST OF FEAR, Blood Song Books, 2019

HALLOWEEN EDITION, Nocturnal Sirens, 2019

HARVEST 2, Blood Song Books, 2020

HOLIDAY SPIRIT, WPC Press 2020

LOCKDOWN PARANORMAL 1 & 2, Black Hare Press 2020

LOCKDOWN SCI FI, Black Hare Press, 2020

LOUISIANA HORROR, Soteira Press, 2020

LOVE IN THE DARK, WPC Press 2020

LOVE, Black Hare Press, 2020

LUST, Black Hare Press, 2020

PRIDE, Black Hare Press, 2020

SHATTERED VEIL, The Great Void Books, 2020

STORIES THAT SING, Havok Publishing, 2020

THE TRENCHCOAT CHRONICLES, Celestial Echo Press, 2020

TWISTED, Medusa Laugh Press, 2017

YEAR ONE, Black Hare Press, 2019

Connect:

Twitter : @chell22_7

Facebook : @Stephaniescissom2019

Facebook Group : @WritingPromptsCritiques

ABOUT THE PUBLISHER

BLACK HARE PRESS is a small, independent publisher based in Melbourne, Australia.

Founded in 2018, our aim has always been to champion emerging authors from all around the globe and offer opportunities for them to participate in speculative fiction and horror short story anthologies.

Connect

Website : *www.blackharepress.com*

Twitter : *@BlackHarePress*